Burke: Sparklers

The books in
the Sparklers *series*
are designed to give
pleasure to young readers
when, having achieved a high
level of confidence, they have
an unrelenting demand for
new and more challenging stories.

Gisela von Radowitz

Felix

Translated by
Alisa Jaffa
Illustrated by
Helme Heine

Burke

First published in the English language 1985

Translated and adapted from *Der verflixte Felix*

CIP data
Radowitz, Gisela von
Felix.—(Sparklers)
I. Title II. Heine, Helme
III. Der verflixte Felix. *English*
IV. Series
833'.914 [J] PZ7

ISBN 0 222 01242 0 Hardbound
ISBN 0 222 01243 9 Paperback

Burke Publishing Company Limited
Pegasus House, 116-120 Golden Lane, London EC1Y 0TL, England.
Burke Publishing (Canada) Limited *Registered Office:*
20 Queen Street West, Suite 3000, Box 30, Toronto, Canada M5H 1V5.
Burke Publishing Company Inc. *Registered Office:*
333 State Street, PO Box 1740, Bridgeport, Connecticut 06601, U.S.A.
Filmset by Graphiti (Hull) Ltd., Hull, England.
Printed in The Netherlands by Deltaprint Holland.

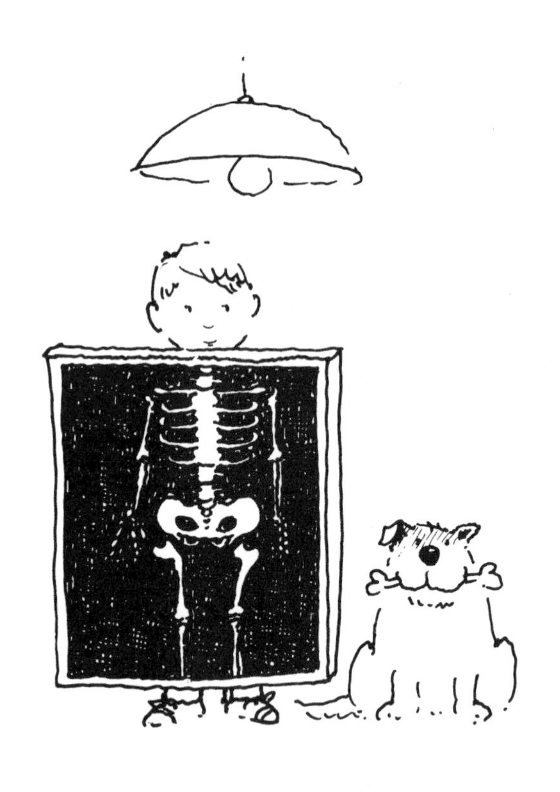

Felix was a big boy.
He'd been going to school
for some time now.
He had brown hair
and his head was filled with dreams.

He had three pairs of trousers,
two old and one new.
In his pocket he kept
three baby teeth,
one fish-hook
and a conker.
He'd given away his stabilizers.
He could ride his bike
without them now.

And he knew how to
spell *garage*.

Whenever he did something bad,
and felt guilty about it,
he would say, "Oh, *flip!*"
And after that
he usually felt a bit better.

Felix had a dog
whose name was Bouncer.
He was greedy, just like Felix.

When Felix felt sad,
he would crawl into Bouncer's basket.
Bouncer understood and comforted him.

Grandma and Grandpa
seemed ancient to Felix.

Grandma had grey hair
and glasses.
She smelled of roast pork
and chocolate pudding.
She knitted jumpers for Felix.
And she had a lot of books.
She often read to him.

Grandpa had a bald head.
And he didn't always have teeth.
But he did have
lots of time for Felix.

Felix had a sister called Martina.
Nearly everyone
dropped the “Mar-”.
Tina was still small enough
to squeeze through the fence
and get apples from next door.

Some days Felix thought she was sweet.
Other days she seemed daft.
She still sucked her thumb,
and sometimes
Felix had to protect her.

Dad was out a lot.
He worked hard.
In the evenings he was
often very tired like Felix.

Dad could be very strict,
but at week-ends
he was like a big brother.
When he laughed,
his eyes smiled
as well as his mouth.

Mum was his mother.
She was a wizard.
She always knew everything,
even before it happened.
Or that's how it seemed to Felix.

One day Felix was very late
home from school.
He'd forgotten
that Mum got worried
if he wasn't on time.

Then he remembered.
"Oh, *flip!*" said Felix.

Mum said to him,
"I feel like
turning you inside out!
Where have you been all this time?"

Felix said,
"I've been catching a burglar.
Burglars must be caught,
you've said so yourself!"
"Maybe I did, but . . . "
" . . . you did say so!"
"All right, Felix.
But I meant real-life burglars.
Those who have done
something bad."

"Well, that's what Kevin did.
He gave Tom a hiding
and that's very bad.
Tom has a black eye now,
and his sleeve's torn.
Besides, he's got a cold.
And it's mean to hit someone
when they've got a cold,
and they're feeling all wobbly."
Mum had to laugh,
although she didn't want to.
"And you had to get
mixed up in it?"
"But Tom's my friend!"
The look on Felix's face
made Mum believe him,
and she couldn't
be cross any more.

"Well," she said uncertainly,
"I was worried,
because there's so much traffic
on that road."
"I'm not a baby any more!"
replied Felix.
But then he was sorry.
He climbed onto Mum's lap,
and put his arms round her neck.
"Sorry," he pleaded
and gave Mum a kiss.

Then Mum wanted to know,
"What was school like?"
"All right," muttered Felix.
But Mum didn't leave it at that.
"Is that all?"
Felix nodded.

The same old question every day—
it never changed.
He thought of the red line
right through the work
in his exercise book,
and below it
in his teacher's neat writing
the words,
"Write this out again!"
Perhaps he could rub them out?

But Mum had already found the page.
"Oh, *flip!*" said Felix.

Her eyes were sharp as an owl's.
Nothing escaped her.
"Felix, oh Felix," she said,
shaking her head.
"Whatever will you do
when you grow up?"
"Look after pigs,"
suggested Felix.
"Like the boy in the story."
Mum didn't think much of that.
Although she was always insisting
on fresh air and exercise.

Felix reminded her,
"But you're always telling me
I'm a little pig.
So I'd know all about it."
Mum changed the subject.
"We'll talk about it
another time."
Looking out of the window,
she said,
"There's going to be a storm.
The sky is quite black."

Immediately Felix asked,
"Is God going to send
thunder into the kitchen
and turn the milk
sour again?"
Mum laughed.
"Funny boy!
I expect so."

Then she unpacked
the shopping
on to the kitchen table.
Sausage, cheese,
fresh bread, cake.
Mmm! How good it all smelled!
Felix was starving.
Couldn't he have just a nibble?

Mum was frowning.
"Silly me!
I've forgotten the butter.
I'll have to run down
again quickly,
before the storm breaks.
Be a pet, Felix,
and put the things
in the fridge for me, will you?
We don't want the thunder
to make them go off."

Felix took the sausage
and was about
to put it away.
The smell wafted
up his nose.
His mouth began to water.
He just couldn't resist it.
"Oh, *flip!*" said Felix.

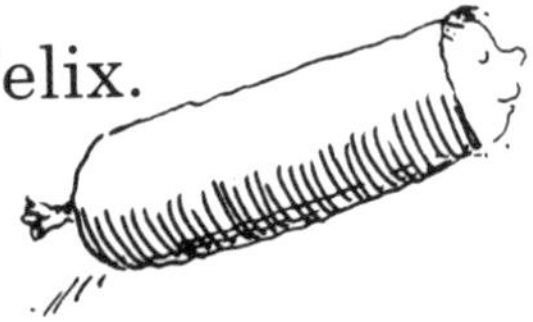

He bit at the sausage,
once,
and again
and then again.
Before he could put it
back in the wrapper,
it had completely disappeared
and his cheeks were bulging.

There was nothing he could do.
Bouncer came snuffling
into the kitchen,
his tail wagging
with excitement.
He looked at Felix expectantly.
"Well, come on then.
Why should you
live like a dog?" said Felix.
And taking a piece of sausage
from his mouth,
he held it out.
Bouncer drooled.
One snap and it was gone.

Mum came back with the shopping.
Felix heard her call, "Bouncer!"
and her voice sounded stern.

She looked from
the empty sausage
wrapper to Bouncer,
and from Bouncer
to the wrapper.
"You wicked, wicked dog!
No dinner for you!"
"Oh, *flip!*" thought Felix.
Bouncer flattened his ears
and crept under Felix's bed.
The world didn't make sense to him.

Felix felt dreadful.
He brooded.
The bread and sausage
Mum had prepared for his lunch
stuck in his throat.
He thought and thought.

What could he do
to make up?
Mum looked at him and asked,
"What's the matter, Felix?"
"Nothing," mumbled Felix.
He could think of only one thing.
He crawled under the bed to
Bouncer and stroked
him lovingly.

"Don't be cross, Bouncer,"
he pleaded.
"I didn't mean to get you into
trouble. I'll make it up to you."

He cleared the dishes in a flash,
and went to his room.
He emptied his piggy bank,
and put the contents in his pocket
along with the three baby teeth,
the fish-hook
and the conker.

Felix called to Mum:
"I'm taking Bouncer for a walk.
It's stopped raining."
"Right you are, dear.
Fresh air and exercise
will do you good.
But mind the traffic!"

At the butcher's on the corner
he bought the biggest sausage
he could see in the shop.
"For you," he said to Bouncer,
and held it under his nose.
Bouncer didn't bear grudges,
so they were both happy again.

4,50

Looking out of the window,
Mum saw Felix
playing hopscotch
on the pavement.
Then she knew
that all was right
with the world once more.

When Dad came home,
Felix had a question for him.
"Listen, Dad, is it true
that thunder is the noise
of God tearing across the sky
in his chariot,
with the wheels
making a terrible din?"
"What makes you think that?"
asked Dad.

"I just do.
But Kevin said
it isn't true,
and that I'd just dreamed it."
"Well, let Kevin
say what he likes.
He might be right.

You see, there are ideas
that are quite important and right
when you imagine them
or dream about them.
But if they really happen,
things get difficult
and sometimes even nasty."

That satisfied Felix.
He spent his life dreaming:
sometimes at night in bed,
sometimes when he was playing,
and sometimes even
in the mornings at school.

"What an imagination that boy has,"
said Dad to Mum.

His imagination was hard at work
that evening. The baby-sitter
was late. Dad and Mum had gone out,
thinking she would soon come.
Felix and Tina were cheerful enough
while it was still light,
but once it got dark
Felix switched all the lights on.
Tina asked him,
"Are you scared?"
She was sitting up in bed.
Felix said crossly,
"Of course not!
Why should I be?"

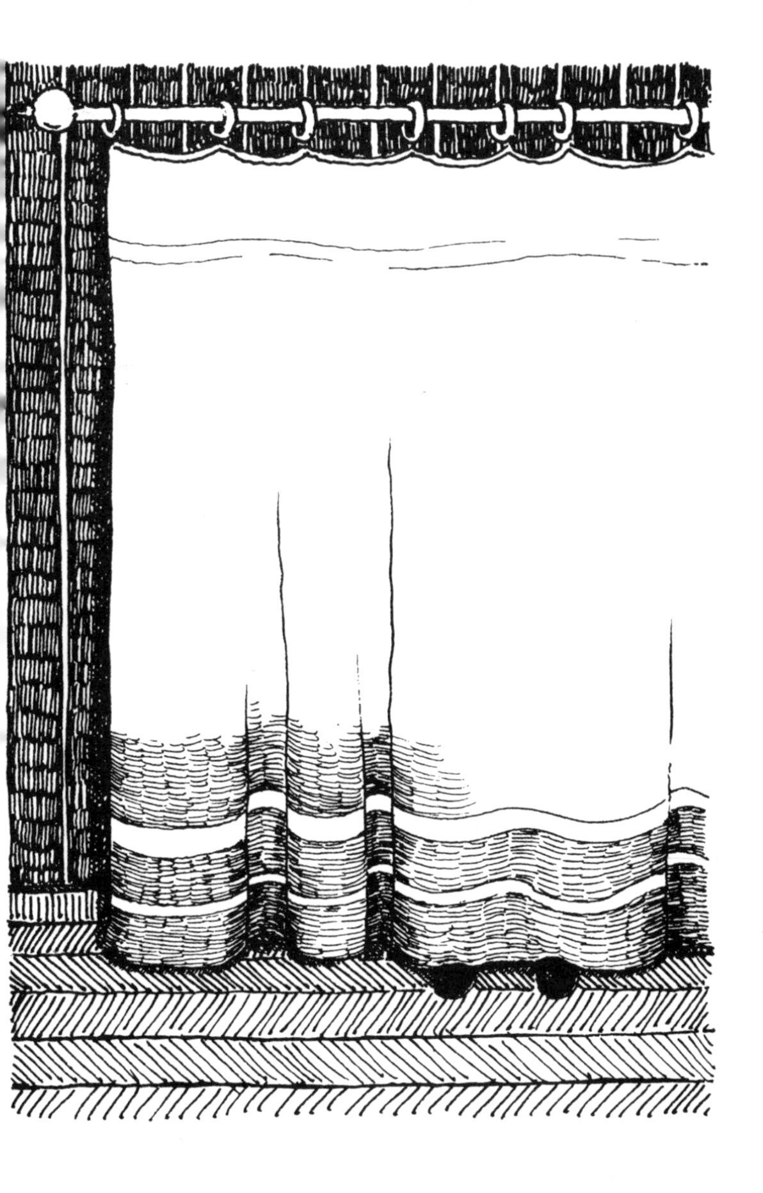

But when the telephone rang
it made Felix jump.
"Who can that be?"
he thought.
"There's no one at home!"
It was Grandpa on the line.
He wanted to know
how they were.
"Fine," Felix insisted.
All of a sudden
he no longer felt scared.

Grandpa asked,
"Will you come
for lunch tomorrow?
You and Tina?
We're having roast pork."
"Sure," said Felix.

Then Grandpa asked,
"And will you bring Grandma
that knitting pattern?"
"O.K.
See you tomorrow, then."
"See you tomorrow."

After Felix put down the phone,
there wasn't a sound in the house.
Bouncer was asleep.
Felix looked at his bed.
Suddenly it seemed huge.
His room was so empty.
He felt lonely.
It was creepy.
What was that?
A burglar
with a torch!

Silly!
Only car headlights.
But listen!
A thief
creeping up the stairs!
Rubbish!
Only Mr. Harper
next door.
And what if
thunder got into
the kitchen again?
"Oh, *flip!*" said Felix.
He really was
getting worked up.
And Tina,
in her cot,
couldn't get to sleep either.
Felix looked across at her.

Suddenly her lower lip
drooped,
and her chin
dropped.
She was howling.

Felix asked:
"What's up, Tinakins?"
Felix felt almost
like crying himself.
"Want to come in your bed,"
howled Tina.
"Come on, then."

Felix was pleased.
He pulled the covers over her,
and wiped away her tears.

She sobbed a little longer,
and snuggled up to him.

When Mum and Dad got home,
all the lights were on in the flat.
Felix had his arm round Tina.
They were both fast asleep,
and looked contented.
Bouncer snored at the end of the bed.

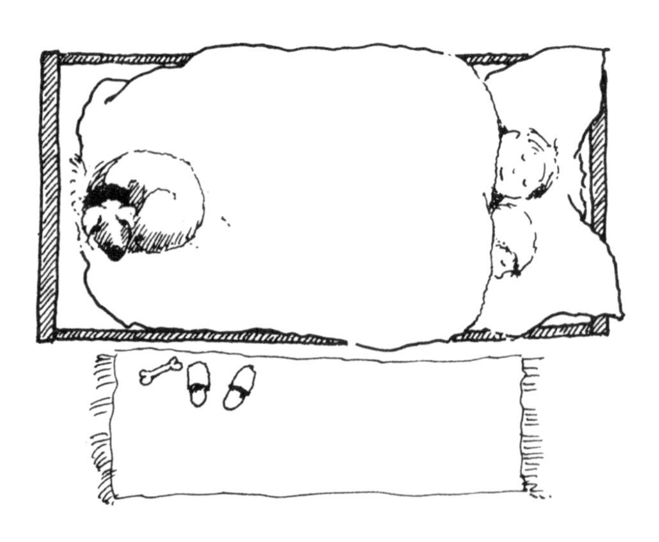

The next day
Dad wanted
to give Felix a treat,
for looking after
Tina so well.
They set off
for a walk.
"Oh, *flip!*" thought Felix.
He didn't want to go.
He wanted to be with Tom.

Tom's uncle was a pilot.
He was visiting Tom's house,
and had asked Tom
to fly with him today.
Felix could just picture
Tom sitting
at the controls.

"Come on," said Dad,
interrupting his day-dream.
"Let's send Clipper
up for a spin."
And, out of nowhere,
he produced Felix's kite.
In a flash, Felix brightened.
He felt the wind
rushing past his ears.
He held Clipper fast
by the crosspiece.
Dad let the line run out
as he ran into the wind.
He called out orders,
"Hold tight!" "Let's go!"
Clipper lashed and pulled.
Slowly the kite spiralled upwards
through the air.

Felix wanted a turn
at holding the line.
It was hard
to keep hold of it.
Clipper climbed higher and higher.
At last, the line was taut.
In his scarlet coat,
Clipper shimmered in the sun
and waved to and fro.
The brightly-coloured
paper tail
danced in the wind.
Felix felt so proud.

Felix was day-dreaming.
He dreamed
Clipper was flying high in the sky.
Along came Tom in the aeroplane.

Tom played with Clipper.
Felix wanted to play, too.
He called out, "I'm coming,"
and spread his arms out like wings
to fly over to join them.
But the wind shook him
to and fro.
He felt quite sick.
"Oh, *flip!*" said Felix.

Felix woke from his day-dream
with a jolt,
and ran to pick up his kite
from the ground.
Then he walked with Dad
through the wood.
The leaves tumbled and rustled
and crackled under their feet.

Felix said,
"They're talking to the wind
and playing *Catch.*"
Dad said,
"Let's play *Catch,* too."
"I'd rather play
Who's afraid of the Big, Bad Wolf?"
replied Felix.

This was a day when Dad did
whatever Felix wanted.
They hid behind
a big pile of leaves.

Someone strolled by
and Felix went,
"Wooooh, wooooh!"
The man was so startled,
he tripped over his own feet.
Felix and Dad giggled.

A woman jumped
when Dad growled
like Bouncer did,
when you took away his bone.

Then Felix snorted
like a steam engine.
Dad clicked his tongue
like a lion-tamer in the circus.

People went,
"Ooooh!" and "Oh my!"
They couldn't see anyone,
so they walked on,
a little faster than before.

At last a small girl
discovered them in the leaves.

"Booh!" she went,
and stuck out
her tongue at them.

Then they burst out laughing
and decided
they'd had enough for one day.
Dad asked,
"Shall we go home now?"
Felix agreed.
"Let's go home," he said.

On the way, they met Tom.
He looked ill.
His face was quite green and yellow.
"Hey, Tom!" said Felix in alarm,
"What's the matter with you?"
"Nothing."

"Are you ill?"
"'Course not."
"What's up, then?"
"Nothing's up."
"Well, didn't you
go flying?"
"Sure, I did."

"Well, what was it like?"
Felix was bursting to know.
Tom pulled a face,
"I was sick as a dog.
What with that wind!"

Tom was in a hurry
to get away.
Felix was silent.
"Funny," he thought to himself.
"This morning I would have done
anything to change places with him."

When they reached the house,
Mum was waiting at the door.
"Hurry up, you dawdlers!
Grandpa and Grandma
are waiting for Tina and Felix.

Mum reminded Felix,
"Don't forget
to wash your hands."
"But they're not really dirty,"
Felix protested.
Mum marched him
into the bathroom, and said,
"Of course not, as usual.

You'll have to be a chimney-sweep
when you grow up,
instead of looking after pigs."

Grandma and Grandpa
lived in the next street.
They were waiting.
Grandma opened the door.
"Did you bring
my knitting pattern?" she asked.
"Oh, *flip!*"
said Felix.

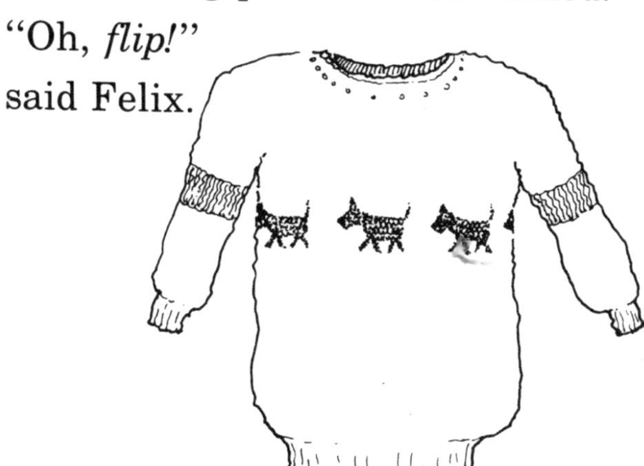

He gasped and clapped his hand
to his mouth.
He'd forgotten!
"But Felix,
you promised
to bring it!
If you make a promise,
you must keep it," said Grandma.

Felix didn't know
what to say.
Grandpa came to his rescue.
"Well, after all,
it's not the end of the world,"
he said.
And he turned to Grandma,
"I'll go and fetch it later."

But Grandma insisted:
"He promised."
"We all forget things sometimes,"
said Grandpa, and winked at Felix.
Felix tried to wink back.
Grandma was still a bit upset.
But lunch was steaming
on the table.
The smell of the roast pork
made everyone feel hungry.
This was no time for arguments.

Then Grandpa took Felix by the hand,
and Felix took Tina's hand,
and she took Grandma's,
and they all marched
round the table
in a line, shouting,
"Which of us is hungry?
Me, me, meeeee!"
until the walls shook.

Suddenly, Grandpa began rummaging
in his pockets. He looked worried.
"What's the matter?"
asked Grandma, as if she knew.
Grandpa mumbled,
"Oh, nothing.
You go ahead and start.
I'll be back in a minute."

But he didn't come.
Where could he be?
When they had almost finished,
he came back
and whispered to Grandma
"Have you seen my teeth
by any chance?"

Grandma laughed.
"No, I haven't."
To Felix it sounded
a bit as if she was
enjoying herself.
"Can't Grandpa chew
without his teeth?" he asked.

Then Felix helped himself
to three more slices
of roast pork.

By the time Grandma had brought
more gravy from the kitchen,
Felix's plate was empty again.
At last, Grandpa reappeared.
He was beaming. He said,
"Children, I've found them.
Now it's my turn to eat."

Grandma chuckled.
"You don't need
your teeth now.
We're having the
chocolate pudding."
When the bowl
had been scraped clean,
Felix went to help Grandma dry up,
without even being asked.
Grandma was very pleased.

Grandma didn't guess
that Felix was standing guard.
He was making sure that
Grandma didn't leave the kitchen.
It was rather awkward.
He had passed Grandpa
his table-napkin with two slices
of roast pork in it!

As they were leaving, Grandpa gave
Tina and Felix some spending money
and said,
"To put in your piggy banks."
But Felix had a better idea.
"I'm going to bury mine
under the apple tree,"
he said.

"If I water it,
it will grow
into a money tree."

As he was going,
Felix turned round one last time.
He placed his finger on his lips
and whispered to Grandpa,
"But you mustn't tell,
or it won't work."

They waved to each other
like conspirators.

Before it got dark,
Felix went out into the garden.
He took a spade and a watering-can
and set to work.
When he came back indoors,
Mum and Dad were horrified.
They hardly recognized him.
His hands and face
were black as pitch.
His socks were soaking wet
and flapped round his ankles.
His trousers were filthy and
his shoes were caked in mud.

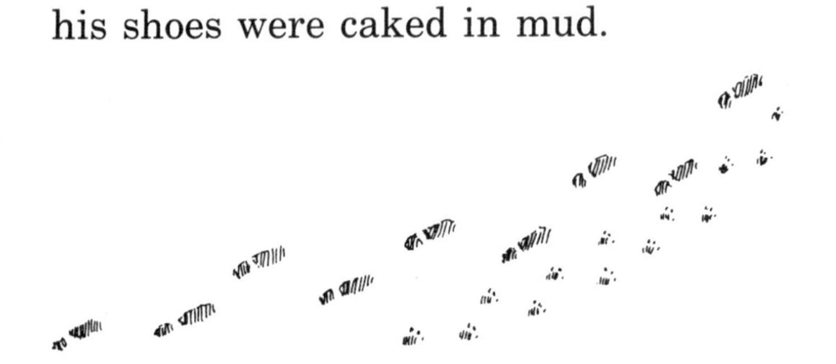

With one voice
Mum and Dad exclaimed:
"Felix, what *have* you been up to?"
"Oh, *flip!*" said Felix.

He didn't know
what to say.
He just stood there
and pouted.

At last, he sniffed and said,
"I'd like to know,
what's the point of being
a big boy like me.
Anything I want to do,
I'm not supposed to do,
and I don't like doing
the things I am allowed to do."

Mum and Dad were lost for words.
They looked at each other,
and then they burst out laughing.
Mum threw her arms round Felix.
"That's *exactly* the point
of being a big boy," she said.

And she hugged and squeezed him
until she was almost as dirty
as he was.